Robert Crewe

Stray verses

1889-1890

Robert Crewe

Stray verses
1889-1890

ISBN/EAN: 9783337282417

Printed in Europe, USA, Canada, Australia, Japan

Cover: Foto ©Andreas Hilbeck / pixelio.de

More available books at **www.hansebooks.com**

STRAY VERSES

1889-1890

ROBERT LORD HOUGHTON

LONDON

JOHN MURRAY, ALBEMARLE STREET

1891

TO

LORD TENNYSON,

WITH GREAT REGARD,

AND GRATEFUL RECOLLECTION OF MANY

HOURS LIGHTENED BY THE SPELL OF HIS GENIUS,

I DEDICATE

THESE FEW VERSES.

THE lines "From Eight to Ten" have been printed in *The World*, and "Easter in Florence" in the *Magazine of Art*.

CONTENTS

x

CONTENTS

PICTURES AND BOOKS

I

ANNA KARÉNINA

WE readers of the older West
> In wonder turn his Eastern page
> Who preaches to a self-loved age
That self-forgetfulness is best :

Figures in grave procession shown,
> No painted things of wire and wood,
> But entities of flesh and blood,
With faiths and passions like our own,

B

And She,—that soul of grace and pride,
 Gripped in the vice of circumstance,
 We hear, as in a breathless trance,
Of how she loved, and erred, and died.

So strong a sister's load to share,
 To eager Love's behest so frail,
 Till all his fires could not prevail
To turn the march of cold Despair,

She learned, as broke the Enchanter's wand,
 The dull reality of things ;
 She beat the cage with bleeding wings,
And burst into the dread Beyond.

And what of us ? unveil who can
 Our own decorous English life,
 The tangle and the secret strife,—
The changeless heritage of man,—

The jangled chords that mar the tune,

    The mad desires, the hopes that die,

    The tragedies that underlie

The laughter of a London June :—

God knows,—who sees us as we are,

    Of contradictions all compact,

    The nobler aim, the baser act,

To hug the yoke, or scale the star :

From fair to foul, from foul to fair,

    Like her, we drift and wander thus :

    God's mercy keep, for her, for us,

Chance of retrieval otherwhere !

II

MILLET AND ZOLA

(" L'ANGÉLUS" AND " LA TERRE.")

AGAINST the sunset glow they stand,
Two humblest toilers of the land,
Rugged of speech and rough of hand,
　　　　Bowed down by tillage ;
No grace of garb or circumstance
Invests them with a high romance,
Ten thousand such through fruitful France,
　　　　In field and village.

The day's slow path from dawn to west
Has left them, soil-bestained, distrest,
No thought beyond the nightly rest,—
　　　　New toil to-morrow :

Till solemnly the " Ave " bell

Rings out the sun's departing knell,

Borne by the breezes' rhythmic swell

      O'er swathe and furrow.

O lowly pair ! you dream it not,

Yet on your hard unlovely lot

That evening gleam of light has shot

      A glorious presage ;

For prophets oft have yearned and kings,

Have yearned in vain to know the things

Which to your simple spirits brings

      That curfew message.

Turn to the written page, and read

In other strain the peasant's creed,

With satyr love and vampire greed

      How hearts are tainted ;

Read to the end unmoved who can,

Read how the primal curse on man

May shape a fouler Caliban

   Than poet painted !

And this is Nature !   Be it so :

It needs a master's hand to show

How through the man the brute may grow

   By Hell's own leaven ;

We blame you not : enough for us

Those two lone figures bending thus,

For whom that far-off Angelus

   Speaks Hope and Heaven.

III

THE ANGEL OF DEATH

(*A PICTURE BY F. A. M. RETSCH.*)

OF all the Powers in Heaven or Hell,
Who stood in grace, or madly fell,
    None wears a countenance like his,
Death's silent Angel, Azrael.

Men shuddering mark him from afar,
High as the hills eternal are ;
    And far behind his locks of flame
Stream, like a dread portentous star :

From canopy of shrouding gloom
Dimly his pallid features loom,—
    Lips locked as are the gates of Hell,
Enclosing words of nameless doom.

But most of all men seek to flee
His eyes' unfathomed mystery,
Deep sunk beneath his lowering brow,
Like caverns by a moonlit sea.

But once the leaves of life are sere,
When draws the darkling Shadow near,
Men, time-bewearied, gaze anew,
And gazing still, forget to fear.--

A trailing glory crowns his head,
A light from Heaven's high portals shed ;
His parted lips are voiceless still,
But smile the benison unsaid.

Meeting those eyes divinely deep,
Eyes sorrow-laden cease to weep ;
Life's night-long fever-dream is done,
God's pitying Angel beckons,--"Sleep."

Of all the Powers in Heaven or Hell,

Who stood in grace, or madly fell,

    None wears a countenance like his,

Death's silent Angel, Azrael.

IV

THE BOOKWORM

(*A Picture by H. S. Marks, R.A.*)

Deep in his oaken elbow-chair,

    In fur-trimmed gown, the old-world Student

Sits toiling with concentrate air,

    And earnest underlip protrudent :

Around him, piled on floor and desk,

    His open books in wealth unstinted, —

Black letter chronicles grotesque,—

    The mellow pages Aldus printed.

A winter sunbeam warms the pane
 Where proudly ramps the lion argent ;
Fleshless and grim, an Afric crane
 Stands facing, like some spectral sergeant :
Bright-plumaged birds of tropic clime
 Lie right and left, a strange collection,
With fruitage of the autumn-time,
 The frugal scholar's spare refection.

On sill and shelf a dusty bloom,
 Sad scandal to industrious Janet :
Dust on the gods from Pharaoh's tomb,
 On figured globe and pictured planet :
A dreamful silence holds the house,
 Time checks his passage down the ages,
And tempts a greatly-daring mouse
 To feast on Pliny's yellowing pages.

Red morning found our student set
    To grapple with some hard construction ;
At midnight chime, intenter yet,
    He vanquished slumber's mild seduction :
He ransacked every age and shore,
    From far Cathay to old Canopus,
To gather up a life-long store—
    New treasures for his *magnum opus.*

He never read Dame Nature's book,—
    The finch's nest, the moldwarp's burrow,—
Nor stood to mark the careful rook
    Peer sidelong down the newest furrow ;
He never watched the warbler dart
    From stem to stem among the sedges,
But, hands behind him, paced apart
    Between his tall-cut hornbeam hedges.

And so his blameless years rolled by,

    To-day the double of to-morrow ;

No wish to smile, no need to sigh,

    No heart for mirth, no time for sorrow :

His forehead wore a deeper frown,

    Eyes grew more dim, and cheeks more hollow,

Till friendly Death one day stepped down,

    And softly whispered, " Rise and follow."

But Fame, victorious maid, resists

    The doom for which gray Time intends us !

Immortal titles crowd the lists

    Which Mr. Quaritch kindly sends us !

'Twixt Drelincourt and Dryden thrust,

    What name confronts you, lone and chilling ?

 " *The works of Gilbert Dryasdust,*

    Quarto : 3 vols. :—old calf :—a shilling."

WITHOUT A NAME

" A daughter . . borne the 3rd of October 1637, about
ten of the clocke at night. Nata et strata. She lyes buryed in
Church with this Inscription.

In libro Vitæ

Tu me

sine nomine scribas."

(*From MS. Family Record in a Prayer Book of* 1638.)

A COMMON record,—scarce the eye

Of any careless passer-by

Might stay to read the how and why.

So trite a doom :

An infant daughter, born to die,—

A nameless tomb.

Save only this,—the line you read
That speaks the parted spirit's need.
Rebels against a hideous creed
　　Of death or flame ;
" Father ! for larger life I plead,
　　Without a name."

Unfathomed mystery of pain !
A wasted hope, a travail vain,
A fruitless birth of vacant brain
　　And nerveless hand ;
The atoms fall to earth again,—
　　A moment's sand.

The aimless stone an idler flings
Strikes on the lake a hundred rings,
They spread to faint imaginings,—
　　At last unseen :
So circling fancy feigns the things
　　That might have been ;

She might have laughed the hours away,

A blushing maiden crowned with May,—

As country dame with locks of gray

    Have filled her part,

Have watched her children's children play,

    Still young at heart ;

She might have fluttered, not so sage,

Caught in St. James's gilded cage,

She might have loved some silken page,

    Or swordsman bold ;

She might have erred,—that courtly age

    Was none too cold.

Enough,—'tis vain to speculate

On buried whims of love or hate,

On unfulfilled decrees of fate

    To stand or fall ;

When dreams are done, we pause and wait,

    " Can this be all ? "

The germ of Life, so vainly sown,

The blade unsprung, the grain ungrown,

In one of yonder worlds unknown,

A meeter field,

May find a harvest all their own,

Of goodlier yield :

For if there be, from sun to sun,

New realms of Being scarce begun,

The Good, as Good, can never shun

That simple prayer ;

Sleep softly, nameless little one,

We leave you there.

SEVEN YEARS

To join the ages they have gone,
   Those seven years,—
Receding as the months roll on ;
Yet very oft my fancy hears
Your voice,—'twas music to my ears
   Those seven years.

Scant the shadow and high the sun
   Those seven years ;
Can hearts be one, then ours were one,
One for laughter and one for tears,
Knit together in hopes and fears,
   Those seven years.

C

How, perchance, do they seem to you,

       Those seven years,

Spirit-free in the wider blue?

When Time in Eternity disappears,

What if all you have learned but the more endears

       Those seven years?

THE INN

But what happens in the world? As though a man journeying to his own country should pass by and rest at a fair inn, and the inn being a delight to him, should abide in it. Man, thou hast forgotten thy purpose : thy journeying was not to this, but through this. "But this is pleasant." And how many other inns are pleasant, and how many meadows? Yet only so as that a man should pass through them.

[Epictetus, *Diss.* II. xxiii. 36, 37.]

Of all the words serenely wise,

That spake the halting Phrygian slave,

Whose eagle doctrine soaring flies

To cheer the fearful,—spur the brave.—

Of all those noble thoughts of his,

    Stamped on an age of blood and sin,

A man may well return to this

    Which teaches of the Wayside Inn.

Beside the road the Inn is set,

    The common way for rich and poor,

And all who pass are freely met

    With greeting glad, and wide-flung door ;

Above the porch, about the wall,

    The crimson roses droop and twine,

In cool arcade, and shadowed hall,

    The clash of dice, the flush of wine,-

And yonder, from the upper room,

    A beckoning of shapely arms,

And purple weft of Tyrian loom

    That vainly veils Neæra's charms.

A garden pleasaunce, all aflame
 With blossomings of East and West,—
The athlete field of race and game,—
 Grottoes to shield the idler's rest,—

And where the myrtles thickest throng,
 Sweet quires unseen succession keep
Of tender-swaying Siren song,
 That burns for love, or sighs for sleep.

Pause, if thou wilt, a summer's day,
 Wisely enjoy the proffered cheer,
But oh, forbear to stretch thy stay
 From week to month, from month to year;

Press on! press on! 'twas not for this
 With wistful hopes thy course began;
An emptied cup,—a loveless kiss,—
 Be these thy gods, O godlike man?

And if in truth thou wilt press on,

    Past ilex shade, and flowery sward,

What then the gods' high benison,

    And what the Traveller's reward?

Some Heraklcian glory-roll?—

    Some errantry by land or sea?--

A Minotaur's unvanquished toll?

    A pale Andromeda to free?—

Nay rather, 'neath a sullen sky

    To bear a useless-seeming load.

Averted looks of passers-by,

    A quenchless thirst, a toilsome road :

Until at last, in rain or sun,

    In lonely vale, or mirthless town,

Soft to thy side approaches One,

    And bids thee lay thy burden down.

An home of fuller brotherhood

    Thus, Traveller, 'tis thine to win,

Merged in the Infinitely Good,

    Oblivious of the Wayside Inn.

ROSES

(A SCENE FROM THE " SENILIA : POEMS IN PROSE," OF IVAN TURGÉNIEFF.)

YEARS since, I know not where, I read the lines ;

Poem and poet both are clean forgot,

Except that, garnered somewhere 'mid the dust

Of boyhood tales, and old disjointed rhymes,

In lilting cadence lingers this refrain :

> *Roses, roses, old-time roses,*
>
> > *Redder to blush, and fresher to blow ;*
>
> *But they bloom no more in the weed-grown closes,*
>
> *The roses of Long-ago.*

And now, in winter, whilst the silent frost

Layer on layer wraps a winding-sheet

About the window mullion, and decks

The pane with cloth of silver, in the room

A single taper flaring yellowly

Makes all the darkness darker, as I brood

Of shadows, crouching near the ingle-nook,

From waking past the border-realm of sleep,

And back again to waking shadow-land.

And through my dream sings on the same refrain :

Roses, roses, old-time roses,

Redder to blush, and fresher to blow ;

But they bloom no more in the weed-grown closes,

The roses of Long-ago.

I seem to stand beside the garden-walk,

Before the low-set window ; black and tall

The towers loom against the flaming west.

There blows a fuller fragrance off the limes,

Hushed from their mid-day murmur, and beneath

Rises a spice of tangled mignonette :

And She is at the window : folded arms,

Head turned to northward, as to bring to view

The fringe of that great sunset; leaning there

In steadfast silence, till the glory fade,

And one by one steal out the waiting stars.

Wide thoughtful eyes, deep-lighted from a soul

Wistful to dare or suffer;—parted lips,

That ask, " What means this Life that lies before ? "

Fair breast that rises rhythmically calm.

Unknowing of the outer passion-storm ;—

Young angel face, whose outlined innocence

Might bow Desire in worship :—silent too

I stand unseen ; I dare not break the charm

Of silence, pilgrim by that silent shrine,

Though Love's wild tumult rages through my heart,

And all his music surges in my ears. . . .

> *Roses, roses, old-time roses,*
>
>> *Redder to blush, and fresher to blow ;*
>
>> *But they bloom no more in the weed-grown closes,*
>
>> *The roses of Long-ago.*

A deeper gloom enshrouds the lonely room,

As darkling shadows flit from wall to wall,

And cross the low-beamed ceiling, from the flame

That flickers in the socket ere it die.

Out in the night I hear the crackling frost,

And here within, in tuneless monotone

Seems crooning on the voice of weary Age :

> *Roses, roses, old-time roses,*
>
> > *Redder to blush, and fresher to blow ;*
> >
> > *But they bloom no more in the weed-grown closes,*
> >
> > *The roses of Long-ago.*

Once more the drifting vapour-clouds unveil

A picture of the Past ;—the homely sound

Of household tasks, and cheerful country toil :—

Two little golden heads close-nestled, eyes

Up-glancing brightly mischievous, a spring

Of brimming laughter welling on the brink

Of lips like flowers, small caressing hands

Tight locked, a chord of eager joyous tones

Attuned divinely; down the corridor

A fearless clash of other little hands

On quavering keys, while through the swaying dance,

That halts and breaks for all that childish care,

A restful music hisses from the urn. . . .

> *Roses, roses, old-time roses,*
>> *Redder to blush, and fresher to blow;*
>> *But they bloom no more in the weed-grown closes,*
>> *The roses of Long-ago.*

High flares the taper like a torch, and dies.

Who groaned there? Speak . . . Close coiled beside my feet

My brave old dog, the last of all my friends,

Lies shivering . . . And I am very cold,

Cold heart and limb, as though some dead cold hand

Were clutching me . . . . and They are dead,—are dead. . . .

> *Roses, roses, old-time roses,*
>> *Redder to blush, and fresher to blow;*
>> *But they bloom no more in the weed-grown closes,*
>> *The roses of Long-ago.*

GONE

(*A Soliloquy.*)

AND thus she leaves me : steals away at dawn.

With needless schemes and childish artifice,

To meet her rather pinchbeck Romeo.

" *They loved as boy and girl, then wilful Fate*

Severed in sport their adolescent years,

But now unites them, ne'er to part again " !

All most romantic, as romances go

In this good nineteenth century of ours,

A theme for Monsieur Guy de Maupassant

Or some such Frenchman of the fleshly school,

The scribes of glorified adulteries,—

But has its dull prosaic side as well.

The details in the manner most approved :

She leaves her jewels, (hers as well as mine,

Which seems to me the opposite of wise,

But always done in novels, I believe),

And on my table just a note, that runs,—

" *This life has been a hell for both of us,*

I cannot bear it longer, so I go.

Good-bye ;—we both have something to forgive."

(All as it should be,—end of Volume Two.)

But stay, to speak in sober earnestness,—

For after all, it has its serious side,

This flight of hers,—I'm willing to believe

That high-flown letter honestly composed.

Well, when a clever girl of twenty-one,

For her own reasons, be they good or bad,—

To help her father, pay her brother's debts,—

Marries a man of nearly thrice her age,

A man with something of a well-known past,

What upon earth does she expect or want ?

The situation, surely, scarce admits

Of poetry ; you hardly can demand

In such a case to meet the Magic Prince,

" And so live happy ever afterwards,"

Just like the tag that rounds the fairy-tale.

" *This life has been a hell for both of us.*"—

What, in God's name, *did* she expect or want ?

Anything money could obtain was hers ;

Society, with freedom to select

Friends of her own, to travel where she wished,

London or country, England or abroad ;—

What more could any woman fairly ask ?

I'm sure enough most women that one knows

Would give an eye for half of such a hell.

Perhaps I spoke in satire now and then,—

But what are words ?—and anything to break

The ice of that impenetrable calm,

To bring the angry crimson to her cheek,

To move the curves about her silent mouth :

Just as I know one sometimes feels impelled

Passing the lilies near a garden walk,

To cut the tallest flower to the ground,

Simply because it stands so white and still

And irritates one somehow ;—as we're told

The good King Arthur bored his Guinevere.

(And now *she's* Guinevere,—with what a cur

To pose as Lancelot ! what an Arthur I !)

Not that I ever struck her. . . . Well . . . a push,

Once,—when she found that letter on the floor,—

And if she needs must bruise her temple vein

(How delicate and blue the veining was,

Just like a touch of Cosway at his best)

Against the caryatid by the fire,

Was I to blame ? . . . . . the purest accident.

   We rubbed on very fairly till he came,

That cousin, with his damned Italian eyes,

Italian airs and graces, and his voice

Worth, if he trained it, two pound ten a week,—

" *Sogno d'amor*," and all the rest of it :—

A vulgar hound I thought him, from the first.

And now she's gone to join him, and to taste

The raptures of a skulking honeymoon

In Norman country town, on Breton coast,

And there await the probable divorce.

Divorce ! no fear ! why, Madam, we are one

Till death do part us, Mother Church has said :

And what if I am good for twenty years ?

How will the long-drawn honeymoon look then

To worn-out woman, discontented man ?

And during all those years of pinch and shame

To touch my money you must beg from me.

But when I die the jointure tumbles in ?

O then she's welcome to the settlements,

For then she may enjoy them if she can :

They're none too large ; I always had in mind

The chance of some such escapade as this,

('The picture even flashed across my eyes

Just as the parson said the binding words)

And so my lawyer beat the jointure down.

Who was it said? . . . . ah! Juvenal I think,—

One's classics get so rusty,—"after all

The most unpleasant side of being poor

Is where it makes you look ridiculous :"

She soon will have a chance of testing that,

If true or not ; the hundred petty slights,

The butcher's swelling clamour for his bill,

The wretched rent unpaid, the shabby clothes.

For what has friend Lothario got a year?

Three hundred? barely ;—not a sixpence more,

And tastes to squander twenty times as much :

Rather a drop from fifty thousand, eh?

" *Sogno d'amor* " will hardly sound so well

Racked on the wheezy lodging-house spinet,—

Half groan, half tinkle, discords high and low,

Lacking the indispensable B flat,—

As murmured through a screen of hothouse flowers,

And rippling down her Steinway's silver scale.

Besides, she had an inborn taste for wealth

Not in a mean or ostentatious sense,

But liked the large existence, liked the power

To give without contriving, liked the feel

Of rich old stuffs, the light of precious stones.

" *A hell*," indeed! she'll find in years to come

New Circles, lower than she ever guessed.

   So far for her : and how about myself?

It's often been my fancy to devise

A kind of mental ledger, side by side

Debit and Credit, such account of life

As strikes one at the moment, good or bad.

   First, then, for Debtor. . . . Well, it's hard to say

What's lost in her. . . . We'll set it down as *x*.

To Creditor, beyond all question, falls

The getting rid of all her kith and kin :

Her half-pay father, angular and dry,

All vile cheroots and prosy Indian lies,—

Of how the tigress charged his elephant,

And how the Sepoys ran at Muddlepore

When he commanded :—*he* will not be missed :

And then her brother, infinitely worse,

The Lovelace of his marching regiment,

Primed with a store of third-hand racing news,

And ever on the prowl for fifty pounds,

Snatched as a greedy mongrel grabs a bone :—

Yes, mongrels, that's their breeding, first and last,

Uncle and aunt, and pauper hangers-on,

A pack of mongrels all,—except herself,

To do her justice, and myself as well ;—

I always looked for quality, be sure,

In horse or woman either . . . well . . . what next ?

There's plenty yet to go to Creditor :

Health ? wonderful, they say, for sixty-three,

Merely a sharp reminder now and then

Of Gout the Avenger : just as quick to pounce

If Ravigotte gets careless ;—and indeed

The race of cooks will soon become extinct,

So different from thirty years ago!

And wine as well,—that '74 to-night

(Perrier-Jouet, beat it if you can)

It hasn't *quite* the flavour others had :

It's curious, that falling-off in things,

Just when one's taste is keenest.

    Sport? of course ·

Though racing isn't what it used to be

In West Australian's or The Dutchman's days,

And even later : what a thrill it was

To watch your colours flashing round the turn,

With Fordham lying third, and sitting still,

And then—" Won cleverly by half a length " !

Now all is altered, half one's friends are dead,

And half the rest are bankrupt : such a mob

Of noisy youngsters jostling near the rails,—

So somehow, for the last ten years or so

I've seldom been to see my horses run.

Hunting? a taste one never fears to lose;

But yet,—it's arrant nonsense to compare

The kind of sport they show you nowadays

With Melton in the fifties: and besides

Of late the weathercock seems glued to east,

And what with months of frost, and weeks of fog,

And hopeless dearth of horses up to weight

With pleasant manners—I'm disposed to doubt

If such a game is worth the candle :—still

There's plenty more to reckon ; works of art,

(Though I admit I've grown a trifle tired

Of Christie's),—books,—and half a hundred more.

Now close accounts : why surely Credit wins?

But stop a moment,—sitting by the fire,

Among my own Penates, I forget

To set to Debtor what may balance all,-

The cursed gossip of the world outside.

It's easy to imagine : in a club

The sudden silence of the window-groups,

The quickly-whispered " Hush !", or " Here he comes ! "

That's bad enough, but still, if that were all . . . .

Men make allowances, or if they don't,

God knows they ought,—why, which of them but owns

A skeleton that waits a chance to burst

Its cupboard,—Gouthière or Sheraton,

But hides the *tête macabre* no less for that?

Ay, but the women! how the vulture heads

Will cluster round the scandal ! one, perhaps

Faintly excusing,—" Come, when such a child

Is mated with a worn-out debauchee,"—

(Yes, that's the phrase to fit your humble servant),

" And loathes her fetters, what can you expect ?

He is the sinner, she the sinned against."

(And yet those worthy dames in some respects

Are larger-minded than one might suppose ;

For if by chance the aforesaid debauchee

Beseeches them to share his fatted calf,

No principle compels them to refuse.)

And then another,—" When a man like this

Marries a girl his granddaughter in age

And trouble follows, let him thank himself:

Three years ago, I think, the wedding was ;

I said it, I remember, at the time,

The fool of fools is still the gray-haired fool."

    Ah ! there's the fatal sting,—a man whose life

Has been, not highly wise or virtuous,—

No patriot, no great philanthropist,

I'm well aware of that,—but all the same

So ordered that to all the lookers-on

It seemed to carry out a settled scheme,

To reach a fixed ideal of its own,—

For such a man,—on dealings of the world

A known authority, a final judge

To arbitrate on points of social law,—

Now to be gibbeted as utter fool,

A laughing-stock for every idiot's tongue !

    I swear to God, if ever I should live

To know her dying where a lifted hand

Would save her,—if I saw her eye to eye

Crawl starving to my feet in beggar's rags,

I'd not forgive her that . . . .

A LONDON WEDDING

UNDER the porch, along the gloomy street,
    Multitudes pressing,
Stare of dull eyes, and pause of idle feet,
    Hearts vaguely blessing:
Garden and square from chestnut and from thorn
    Snow-blossoms shedding,
Sultry and gray the sunless London morn
    Welcomes the wedding.
Here in the church, the blank uncomely aisle
    Whispers with greetings,
Half-uttered jest and veiled reproving smile,
    Languorous meetings;
High above all, the organ rises loud
    Swelling in thunder,

Silent at last, the gay unthinking crowd
  Opens asunder.
See how she comes, "the toast of all the town,"
  Daintily slender,
Little head high, but eyes bent shyly down,
  Trustful and tender :
Soft-flowing lace and shimmering of pearl
  Wears she divinely,
Soft too her train's inimitable swirl,
  Broidered so finely.
See where he waits, the lover for his own,
  Royally daring,
Once he be hers, a Cæsar's lofty throne
  Not worth the sharing :
They two alone, and nearer none shall stand,
  Father nor mother,
They two alone are plighting hand to hand,
  Either to other.

" Ah, but the key they miserably miss,
        Hearts never mated ;
Surely to earn the day that gives us this,
        Time was created ?
Sundered, the years fled empty as a dream,
        Aims were the vainest ;
Here is the purpose and the hour supreme,
        Life's meaning plainest."

Here let the World's interminable din
        Hush for a breathing,
Here let the cauldron of the city's sin
        Rest from its seething :
Rest, O sad players, from your dreary parts,
        Sated and scornful ;
Rest for a moment, disappointed hearts,
        Tearlessly mournful.
Long summers since,--invulnerable Man,
        Coldly regretful,--

Mind you of how the old romance began,

    Fevered and fretful?

Wavering hopes, and chill unreasoned fears,

    Daring, and knowing :—

Say, is her grave quite hidden by the years,

    Weeds overgrowing?

You, fairest Dame,—a web of petty schemes

    Jealously twining,—

Once on a time across your blameless dreams

    Dawn-rays were shining :

Eyes to meet yours unalterably true,

    Lips to adore you ;

Spare, if you can, a prayer for the Two

    Kneeling before you.

Far down the years, when eyes are growing dim,

    Loveliness waning,

What from to-day shall then for her, for him,

    Yet be remaining?

Sullen reproach, and querulous regret,

    Sorrow and scorning ?—

Rather—leal hearts, feet resolutely set

    Straight for the morning.

Close we the book, and bravely thrust aside

    Life's hidden pages ;

Thus may they stand, the Bridegroom and the Bride,

    One through the ages.

A LONG FAREWELL

A LONG Farewell! To-night we go
From mists that chill, and gales that blow ;
    And follow to a stormless clime
    The promise of a sunnier prime,
Forth of these shores of northern snow.

And facing that Hesperian glow,—
As Fancy's currents ebb and flow,
    They range themselves in halting rhyme,—
        A long Farewell.

What thoughts come flooding to-and-fro !—

The balanced beam of Yes and No,—

    Passions of earth, and dreams sublime,—

    Sorrows,—unhealed till weary Time

Bids Then, and Now, and Long Ago,

        A long Farewell.

A WET SUNSET IN SOUTH AFRICA

Across the waste of dreary veldt,
  Unmarked by hut, or knoll, or hollow,
The lifeless mountain's arid belt
  Trends southward, far as eye can follow.

A fitful rain is dripping still,
  Close to the plain the swifts are skimming;
The thirsty soil has drunk its fill,
  And left a thousand pools a-brimming.

The west is rapt from sight and sense,
  Lost in a haze of fairy yellow ;
A sadness, born we know not whence,
  Falls with that light divinely mellow :

E

Where hangs unseen the guiding Cross,
 The lightning's magic veil is lifting,
Clouds like Atlantic billows toss,
 From summit on to summit drifting ;

Eastward, a cold unearthly sheen
 Of mists fantastically riven,
All steel and silver damascene,
 Bright armour for the hosts of heaven.

Unbidden memories of home
 The stranger landscape seem to hallow,—
The tender touch of English Crome
 On Norfolk broad, and stream, and shallow,—

A dream of looming towers that crown
 A northern city's smoke and shadow,
Where Lincoln Church looks stately down
 On flooded fen and steaming meadow.

One moment,— off the vanished sun
    A redder fire of glory flushes,
The pools grow rosy one by one,
    The pallid east in answer blushes :

Another,— half the glow is gone,
    The near and far in shade are blended,
Black-plumaged night flies swiftly on,
    The curtain falls,—the dream is ended.

SNOW AND SUN

HERE in the snow-land,—crouch and shiver,—
   A gray dead sky, and the world afreeze,
Grinding ice in the brim-full river,
   A shriek of the wind in the starving trees :
O for an hour of a reef-girt island,
   In the quivering noon of its tropic calm,
Shell-strewn shore, and untrodden highland,
   Dense mimosa, and high-crowned palm !

There in the sun-land,— tossing, turning,—
   Fire-blown air, and the glare of sand,
A furnace-vault in the zenith burning,
   Heart out-wearied, and failing hand :

O for a breeze through the cordage sighing,

   Salt in your teeth of the cool sea-foam,

A wrack of clouds, and the pale sun dying,—

   Face set straight for a northern home !

IN MEMORIAM

ROBERT BROWNING, DIED 12TH DECEMBER 1889.

THE tale of how you found the promised rest
Flashed fast from north to south, from sea to sea,
My father's friend, all friendliness to me,
Dear Scholar-Poet,—ever-welcome guest :
And gone you are to seek your loved-one's breast,
Sped your free soul from Italy the free,
Soul never flinching from the dim To Be,
Nor doubting of the Good,— and thus, 'tis best.
'Tis best,—and I, six thousand miles away
From your and Nelson's Abbey [1] arched in gloom,

[1] At the battle off Cape St. Vincent, "Nelson . . . gave orders
for boarding . . . it was done in an instant, he himself leading the
way, and exclaiming—' Westminster Abbey, or victory ! ' "—Southey's
Life of Nelson.

Hear through the surge that thunders on the bay

An echo of your verse's [1] roll and boom

That doubly sanctifies Trafalgar day,—

And waft this Afric leaf to reach your tomb.

[1] " Home Thoughts from the Sea."

CAPETOWN, 1889.

TO MY SISTERS

WITH A VOLUME OF TRANSLATIONS FROM BÉRANGER.

TAKE these few verses, all too idly done

In English,—pondering the weary while

Of English fields, and faces, and the smile

Of those we loved whose golden sands have run,

Of hopes that flowered not, duties scarce begun,—

Along the changeless banks of tawny Nile,

Or scanning Karnak's immemorial pile

Lit with the glory of the dying sun.

My Poet sang them in a different scene,

Bright child of Paris, blent of joys and fears,

He loved, and sinned, and suffered, most serene

When winning most the poor man's mirth or tears :

Firmer perchance his footsteps would have been

With hands like yours to guide him down the years.

FOOL'S PARADISE

THE joyous Paradise of Fools
    Has space to spare for young and old ;
    There Love is infinitely bold,
And there his altar never cools :

For neighbour oars on silent pools,
    For comrade feet in meads of gold,
The joyous Paradise of Fools
    Has space to spare,—for young and old.

But once we leave its fairy Rules
    For Reason's realm of doubt and cold,
    Our eyes may never more behold
That dear despair of all the Schools,
The joyous Paradise of Fools.

DOWN THE STREAM

LOVE ! It began with a glance,
   Grew with the growing of flowers,
Smiled in a dreamful trance,
   Recked not the passage of hours :
Our passion's flood rose ever,
   Flowing for her and me,
Till the brook became a river,
   And the river became a sea.

Grief! It began with a word,
  Grew with the winds that raved;
A prayer for pardon unheard,
  Pardon in turn uncraved;
The bridge so easy to sever,
  The stream so swift to be free!
Till the brook became a river,
  And the river became a sea.

Life! It began with a sigh,
  Grew with the leaves that are dead;
Its pleasures with wings to fly,
  Its sorrows with limbs of lead:
And rest remaineth never
  For the wearier years to be,
Till the brook shall become a river,
  And the river become a sea.

THE BIRD

" He shall rise up at the voice of the bird." *Ecc.* xii. 4.

THE voice of the bird,—in a primrose lane,
   When my love and I were young ;
Standing together to catch again
   The story the lark had sung.

The voice of the bird,—the answering thrills
   Of lovers passion-pale,
Under the moon, to the longing trills
   Of the tireless nightingale.

The voice of the bird,—a livid sky,
    A tempest of whirling leaves,
To hearts that sever, a long good-bye
    From the swallows that line the eaves.

The voice of the bird,—when a spirit wings
    Its return to Him who gave,
And the redbreast sits and gaily sings
    On the brink of an open grave.

I TOLD YOU SO

Down by the sea, where the cliff is high,
 There, where the oleanders blow,
We walked at evening, you and I,
 Speech was eager, and steps were slow :
 You were my love,—and I told you so.

Doubt came down like a breath that blew
 Straight from the far horizon snow :
Eyes reproachfully turning, you.—
 " Men are ever alike, I know :—
 To mistrust that I love, when I told you so!"

It is over now, and I might have known,

     From the very first, how the day must go :—

He was the better man, I'll own :

     So I spoke once more, and your Yes was No :

     And the world consoles with—" I told you so ! "

COUSINS

He

ONCE, dear, when you and I were young,
And tight the silver cord was strung,
We caught the roses Fortune flung,—

    When we were young :

She

Now, dear, that you and I are old,
Your love is lead, that then was gold,
Your wide-sung praises leave me cold,-

    Now we are old.

F

Once, dear, when you and I were fools,

We scoffed at formal Fashion's rules,

Through mad Julys and frolic Yules,

  When we were fools :

He

Now, dear, that you and I are wise,

And done with childhood's vanities,

Why, tell me, shrink our meeting eyes,—

  Now we are wise?

MERE WASTE OF TIME

A Troubadour's Dedication

MERE waste of time ! Such rhymes as these,

A careless task for hours of ease,

  No lofty thought, no fancy new,

  No hope to emulate the few

For whom grow green the laurel trees ;

Light as the foam that flecks the seas,

Fitful as summer's sunset breeze,

  As transient as morning dew,—

            Mere waste of time !

Poor guilty drone before the bees !

From tones that chide, and looks that freeze,

Impenitent I turn to you,

Your clustered hair and eyes of blue,

And whisper, " Is my toil to please

Mere waste of time ? "

THE WHITE BUTTERFLY

(There is a superstition that when a white butterfly settles on a
girl's dress, her lover is thinking of her.)

You sit demure, a silhouette

 Against the rosy-flooded west ;—

See, on your skirt's soft violet,

 That white-winged butterfly at rest :

How rustic *Dolly's* artless breast

 Would flutter fast, if you were she !

She'd whisper, "One that loves me best

 Is thinking now of me,—of me !"

Ah well! such quaint beliefs as those
    Can't meet a scientific stare,
And Darwin doubtless plainly shows
    Why insects settle here or there.
Yet some of us may long to share
    The faiths and hopes of simpler men ;
And folk-lore tales, Miss Golden-Hair,
    Are wondrous truthful—now and then !

YOUR SONGS

I LISTEN to the songs you sing,
    Grave elegies or gay romances,
And straight my limping thoughts take wing
    To join you in a world of fancies ;
To fly with you through time and space,
    Beyond this life of mortal seeing,
New creatures of a changeful race
    Your voice has ushered into being.

And on this phantom stage of yours,
    Be farce or tragedy the drama,
One guiding motive still endures
    Through all the shifting panorama :

Let love be crowned, or hope be mocked,

    June or December rule the weather,

Your fate and mine rest interlocked,

    To play our destined parts together.

How softly falls "the dying day,"

    As you, that magic slumber ending,

" *Across the hills, and far away,*"

    Close to my side your steps are wending;

How glow, like yonder Ayrshire sun,

    The passion-laden lines I utter,

While you are " *Mary Morison,*"

    And I the Bard beneath your shutter.

But ah! sometimes your songs remind

    Of lilies stained and roses blighted,

That Beauty is not always kind,

    That falsehood thrives, and faith is slighted:

How *Vivien* wove the charm unseen
    For Merlin where the oaks were shady,
Or how "*the River ran between*"
    The Soldier and his ruthless Lady.

And thus, and thus, the measures sway,
    From Tosti's languid southern slumbers,
To Breton ballad, Scottish lay,
    Or lofty Wagner's pregnant numbers :
But be their outcome laugh or sigh,
    Their moral cynical or tender,
You queen it through them all, whilst I
    My poor identity surrender.

For all my inmost fibres thrill
    Responsive to your music's changes,
As answered to Amphion's quill
    The rocks on purple Theban ranges :

You strike a solemn chord that brings
  Me nigh to poet, saint, or hero,—
Till soon some flippant *scherzo* flings
  My fine ambitions down to zero.

But how reduce to common life
  Such high and mystical devotion?
How (speaking plainly) take to wife
  The figment of an hour's emotion?-
Well, after all, one must suppose
  (And I for one would not upbraid him)
That Petrarch's self made love in prose,
  And Bach without a fugue to aid him.

FOUR LOVERS

I

IN SPRING

Across the lawn, adown the walk,

We carried our familiar talk,

By paths yew-shaded :

The rain was past, but dewy yet

It left your hand, this violet

Which here lies faded.

We scanned the sleeping lily-beds,

The daffodils' unrestful heads,

The primrose border :

Below the din of nesting rooks,

You reckoned up your favourite books

In gracious order.

We walked the fields with *Lily Dale*,

We sighed that *Hetty* spurned her pail

In wayward fancy,

We traced *The Moonstone's* deadly clue,

And climbed the tempting wall with you,

Dear candid *Nancy*.

Of graver prose you loved the best,

You'd bind across Macaulay's breast

The bluest ribbon ;

Thought Carlyle execrably rude,

Liked Emerson, were charmed by Froude,

And hated Gibbon.

Was it that sacrilegious name ?—

That just in view the Abbey came

Between the birches ?—

Well, anyhow, 'twas writ by Fate

That you and I should join debate

On creeds and churches.

I needs must strut with sceptic airs,
Display my gimcrack London wares,
    " Last lights were truest ;
How could the Gospel stand the shocks
Of Hume's most time-worn paradox,
    Of Renan's newest ? "

I see your look as yesterday :
Your father's guest must end his say,—
    Nor kindle passion ;
You bit your lip, and shook your head,
Smiled at yourself as " country-bred,—
    Quite out of fashion."

And I ?—well, vanity was blind
To what emotions thronged your mind
    That fateful morning ;
Some disappointment, underset
With pity, just a faint regret,
    But most of scorning.

I sought to trench on tenderer ground,
To hint at sentiments profound,
        But no, I could not :
That springtide walk had snapped the chain,
I might not weld its links again,
        And you,—you would not.

And twenty-one is wrapped in pride,
And so it fell I never tried
        To crave re-hearing ;
Was there, had you but cared to know,
Some kind of manlier self below
        My poor veneering ?

Ah me ! the fleetfoot years have sped,
And never more your steps can tread
        That old-time garden :
Some day, perchance, 'mid other flowers,
I, mindful of those squandered hours,
        Shall win your pardon.

II

IN SUMMER

I MET you all the Season long,

    I loved you from its chill beginning ;

Who else could show, throughout the throng,

    A smile so soft, or eyes so winning ?

Diana in the early Park,—

    At every ball you reigned as Venus ;—

And right and left was heard remark,

    We soon should settle it between us.

An Ascot week,—a cloudless dream ;—

    An idle day at Burnham Beeches ;—

An evening's dawdle down the stream

    Along the shady Clieveden reaches ;—

And often, spite your chaperon's qualms,

    We found it far too hot for dancing,

When tall conservatory palms

    Bore witness to our light romancing.

One serpent thought, alas ! must wind
Its path within our Eden's pleasure ;
It troubled my superior mind
To contemplate your thoughtless leisure :
Amusement had a spell for you,
Which, so I felt, was simply shocking ;—
I always thought a tinge of blue
Improved a charming woman's stocking !

And so, with airs of soberer age,
I tried some well-intentioned teaching :
At last, one day, I reached a stage
Of quite unwarrantable preaching :
"Shallow,"—you set your face like steel ;
"Sheer waste of time,"—you flushed carnation ;
"Frivolity,"—you stamped your heel,
And then,—defined the situation.

" A man, it seemed, found various ways
    Of culture deep and self-improvement ;
Might 'stand a dash in Brighton A's,'
    No less than head a Temperance movement :
Might (said ill-natured folks) escape
    The House of Commons' midnight humours,
To gather off a sinuous tape
    The very last Newmarket rumours.

" Woman's existence, if you please,
    Must ripple down a quieter channel ;
To mind her soul, and keep her keys,
    And regulate the Christmas flannel :
Since School Boards knocked at every door,
    To read three hours a day were prudent ;
Part ' Little Sister of the Poor,'—
    Part Lady-help,—part Newnham Student !

" My Politics?   a trivial game

     Of Outs and Ins, of jobs and places ;

My Letters?   just a civil name

     For stolen thoughts and borrowed graces :

What if myself should indicate

     One generous aim, one wise ambition,

Before I dared again to prate

     My platitudes of woman's mission ? "

And so I left you : all amaze,

     Struck dumb by that contemptuous sally,

As though a lava stream should blaze

     Along some smiling Devon valley ;

I felt each syllable that fell

     Come burning from the heart within you :

I never loved you half so well

     As when I knew I could not win you !

Since then your fruitful life has shown
    What mind indeed is worth possessing;
Each year that life has ampler grown,—
    A wider work, a higher blessing:
How right you were that day! but I,
    To whom the world does not seem kinder,
Dream of that far-away July,
    And ask, was ever Cupid blinder?

III

IN AUTUMN

Low in the valley the wreathing mist
    Tells its tale of the year grown old;
A slanting beam on the hill has kissed
    The beeches' russet, the birches' gold:

As I stand and gaze from the faded grass
    Up to the faint October blue,
Line above line the wildfowl pass,
    Winging westward from me to you.

Lady mine, is it fault of mine,
    Or deed of yours, that we stand asunder?
Fanciful Chance, or high Design?—
    Do you ever spare me a thought, I wonder?
Pity, perhaps, for a life forlorn,-
    Fortune of war as a queen bewails :
And ever so little a shade of scorn,—
    A woman's scorn for the man who fails.

Lady mine, to your windswept home,-
    Ice from the north, and balm from the west,—-
Let never a blast of memory come
    To trouble the smooth of your perfect breast ;

Never a flying shadow of blame
  The fearless breadth of your brow shall cross ;
Say that we played at a summer's game,--
  Mine the blunder, and mine the loss.

Perhaps at your "Yes" I tried to snatch
  Too soon for the pride that your spirit owns ;
Perhaps my ear was too dull to catch
  Your character's subtlest semitones :
But listen,—be light or heavy the load,
  Summer or winter, early or late,
I shall watch your footsteps down the road,
  Till you turn and beckon, I stand and wait.

IV

IN WINTER

The crimson sun has reached the ridge,
I linger on the oaken bridge
  Fine-filigreed with yestern snow ;

O'er distant wood and rolling park
Film upon film steals on the dark,
    And dulls the borrowed eastern glow.

No faintest sigh of northwind stirs
The canopy of arching firs,
    The alder-branches half-revealed ;
A rabbit moves the crispening brake.
The wildfowl flighting from the lake
    Wheel high, and circle for the field.

Six months agone the fern was green,
The alders wore their summer sheen,
    Close to our feet the wildfowl came :
'Twas here I lingered long with her,
And watched the arrowy kingfisher,
    A gleam of hundred tinted flame.

"Come close, my love, and closer yet,—
One moment never to forget
    Through all the looming years of pain ;
It wrongs not you, nor him, to kiss
Eyes never more to melt like this,
    Lips never to be mine again."

In all the dreary month of snows
Through yonder ice-locked mere there flows
    The never-ceasing central stream :
And through this colder life of mine
Wanders a rivulet divine,—
    The rapture of that vanished dream.

A WILTSHIRE LEGEND

Olive, one of the daughters and co-heiresses of Sir Henry Sherington of Lacock Abbey, being in love with John Talbot of Salwarpe, Worcestershire, contrary to her father's wishes, "discoursing one night with him from the battlements of the abbey church, said she 'I will leap downe to you.' Her sweetharte replied he would catch her then : but he did not believe she would have done it. She leapt down, and the wind, which was then high, came under her coates, and did something break the fall. Mr. Talbot caught her in his armes, but she struck him dead ; she cried for help, and he was with great difficulty brought to life again. Her father thereon told her since she made such leapes, she should e'en marrie him."—Aubrey's *North Wilts*.

UNDER the lee of the Bowden steeps,
    By the willowy banks of Avon,
In sunlit meadows the Abbey sleeps ;

And the elm trees' lengthening shadows fall
On mullioned window and ivied wall,
   And lawns like a churchman shaven.

Sleeps the Foundress under the stone,
   Where she ruled---"COMITISSA SARVM,
ABBATISSA,"—in years agone ;
And the rhyming monkish hexameters
Dwell on the graces that once were hers,-
   "VIRTVTVM PLENA BONARVM."

Centuries three had she lain at rest
   'Neath the stone where her name is graven ;
The nuns were scattered to east and west,
For tower and cloister and banqueting-hall,
Stern Sir Harry he held them all,
   And the meadows by winding Avon.

And youth was astir, and love was awake,
    Where the saintly dead lay sleeping;
All for the Lady Olive's sake,
Lady Olive so daintily fair,
With her sea-blue eyes, and her tangled hair,
    Like corn that is ripe for the reaping.

Young John Talbot he loved her well,
    Lover was never a truer:
But a lover's tale he scarce might tell,
For when lands are lost, and gold has been spent,
Though his blood be the best between Thames and
        Trent,
    What father will welcome a wooer?

Long she lingered, that night in June,
    On the high-set battlement leaning,
Pale in the light of the rising moon:

And she sighed to her gallant far below,

As Juliet sighed to her Romeo,

    A message of tenderest meaning.

"See," she murmured, "the moon is high,

    Her path is on Avon river;

It were sweet, O my love, by her light to fly,

Through brook and coppice, o'er meadow and down,

Away to the gates of London town,—

    Two hearts to be one for ever!"

And she gazed to the depth, and she did not shrink,

    Though she heard her heart-beats quicken,

And she leapt from the high-set battlement's brink,

Wafted down on the wings of love,

As drops from the nest a silvery dove

    To her mate that the falcon has stricken.

Young John Talbot was stout of arm,

    Courage and heart unshaken ;

He clasped her and held her safe from harm,

But he slipped and fell on the pitiless stone,

Lay at her feet with never a groan,

    In a slumber no kiss could awaken.

Clear rang out Lady Olive's call,

    Startled the bloodhound sleeping :

Lights came flashing in chamber and hall,—

Roused Sir Harry and all his men,—

Stern Sir Harry grown gentle then,

    At sight of his darling a-weeping.

'Twas an hour ere the gallant could open his eyes

    On his love so faithful and daring,—

Read in hers that he'd won his prize :

Swore Sir Harry,—"The maiden's leap

Has earned her for you, to take and to keep,

   She's a favour that's worth the wearing!"

Such is the legend of days gone by,—

   Worthy a worthier poet :

But well-a-day! and a man may sigh,

Sigh for the days of brave Queen Bess,

When a lady's "Yes" was verily yes,

   And she'd peril her neck to show it!

CUPID'S GRAVE

HERE Cupid rests within his narrow cell;

　　Never did friend deserve a record better:

Had he a fault?—Liked he the chase too well?

　　Forgive him,—he was but a Gordon setter.

Must all that grace and gentle kindness die,

　　And Love, my Cupid, hopelessly regret you?

Well,—we shall learn the secret by and by;

　　Till then, sleep sound, and we shall not forget you.

EASTER IN FLORENCE

'Twas Eastertide of Eighty-Nine,—
    That time of rest for every nation,
When weary legislators pine
    For ten brief days of relaxation :
Her finest crown Queen Florence wore,
    Produced her fairest April weather,
In welcome to the Travellers four
    Who roamed her storied streets together.

We wandered through the glorious fane
    Which seems to guard the city sleeping :
Past still St. George, through sun and rain
    His steadfast knightly vigil keeping :

Beside the Strozzi walls we strolled,

    And grumbled at Palotti's prices,

But somehow found ourselves consoled

    By Doney's *déjeûners* and ices!

We stood where choirs at twilight sang,

    We watched the flying Dove's ignition,—

A famous peg on which to hang

    A grand discourse on superstition!—

Perhaps those simple souls might teach

    Lessons as high as we could set them,

And if they're striving heaven to reach

    Their own strange road,—by all means let them!

We drove along, to sound of bells,

    Past villa walls and marble fountains,

To where the white Carthusian cells

    Peer out towards the snow-capped mountains:

On Fiesole's historic crest
    The thrushes sang a Paschal chorus,
While, lighted from the lurid west,
    The teeming plain rolled wide before us.

We paced through frescoed council-halls,
    Dim with the dust of buried ages ;
We lingered near the gorgeous walls
    Where winds the train of Eastern Sages :
And thoughtfully the cells we trod
    Which held within their narrow border
The Prior who preached the wrath of God,—
    Stern Quixote of a Sacred Order !

The echoes of a bygone strife
    Seemed surging round the dark Bargello ;
Marble and bronze sprang fresh to life
    Beneath the wand of Donatello

" *Night* " seemed to sleep, and " *Dawn* " to wake

Behind the walls of old St. Lawrence,—

There hung a spell we would not break

About our Eastertide in Florence.

We passed where Rubens' beauties lay,—

Never a rag their buxom limbs on,—

To see our courtly P. R A.,

Resplendent in his robes of crimson :

Past canvases, by years undimmed,

From Antwerp, Nuremberg, and Cadiz,

To mark how nobly Titian limned

Grey senators and highborn ladies.

From grave Mantegna's glowing reds,

To soft Correggio's milder graces ;

From Botticelli's down-cast heads,

To bright Andrea's smiling faces ;

And that good Friar, to whom alone
    Of mortal men was spirit given
To pierce the veil that shrouds the Throne,
    And paint the golden courts of Heaven.

Silent we stood, in deepest awe,
    Where Raphael's hand has set for ever
The whirlwind Israel's prophet saw
    In vision by the captives' river:
Silent, where sits in loveliest guise
    The wistful Virgin Mother, leaning
To watch her wondrous Infant's eyes,
    Enkindled with divinest meaning.

Now turn the page, and seek the round
    Of daily pleasures, pains and duties :—
It's good to stand on English ground,—
    A London summer has its beauties ; ··

Time mows away at memory's flowers,

    He holds their perfume in abhorrence,

Freely we'll yield him most of ours,

    But not that Eastertide in Florence!

TO DORIS

" Ah ! conservez-moi bien tous ces jolis zéros
　　Dont votre tête se compose.
　　Si jamais quelqu'un vous instruit,
　　Tout mon bonheur sera détruit
　　Sans que vous y gagniez grand'chose."

IF, my Doris, I should find,

That you seem the least inclined

To explore the depths of Mind,

　　　　Or of Art,

Should such fancies ever wake,

Understand, without mistake,

Though our hearts (perhaps) might break,—

　　　　We must part.

I'd as soon your little head

Should be lumbered up with lead,

As with learning, live or dead,

      And with brains ;

I have really doted less

On its outline, I confess,

Than the charming Nothingness

      It contains.

No, suppose by hook or crook

People try to make you look

At some tiresome crabbed book,

      Mind you don't !

If they hint you ought to know

Sophocles or Cicero,

Bacon, Goethe, or Rousseau,

      Say " *I won't !* "

Do you think the summer rose

Ever cares or ever knows

By what law she buds and blows

On the stem ?

If the peaches on the wall

Must by gravitation fall,

Do you fancy it at all

Troubles them ?

Then, as sun or rain is sent,

And the golden hours are spent,

Be unaskingly content

As a star :

Yes, be ever of the few

Neither critical nor blue,

But be just the perfect You

That you are !

IN AN ALBUM

Your empty page! "A verse, a skit,
A tuneful trifle, deftly writ;"—
   I feel as one who writhes with gout
   The morrow of a drinking-bout :
When reason reels, and senses flit.

O for a shaft of Sydney's wit,
Or Jerrold's gibe, that burned and bit :—
   Though no uncourtly line must flout
                 Your empty page.

" Poeta nascitur, non fit : "

(A trite quotation, I admit)

    Its bearing plain,—" Why single out

    Prosaic folks— ? "—Hurrah ! a shout

Of triumph !—" Why ? "— I've covered it

        Your empty page !

FROM EIGHT TO TEN

In Rotten Row, from day to day,
    The hardy riders lightly muster,
Who love the scent of silvery may,
    The bright laburnum's golden cluster :
Benevolent Hygeia smiles
    Promise for years beyond our ken,
On those who do their dozen miles
    In Rotten Row, from eight to ten.

When d'Orsay ruled, our fathers braved
    In glossier garb all sorts of weather,
The ladies' flowing habits waved,
    And headgear bore an ostrich feather ;

Who now performs a caracole?

    We're clad to climb a Perthshire glen .

There's nothing of the *haute école*

    In Rotten Row, from eight to ten !

Once, sturdy cob of fourteen-two

    So short of leg, so deep of shoulder.

You grazed where Channel breezes blew

    Their keenest breath on moor and boulder ;

As o'er the cocksfoot tufts you bent.

    No notion ever crossed you then

Of trotting Seventy per Cent

    Up Rotten Row, from eight to ten !

You, highborn steed, more priceless still.

    We welcome you, a " blithe newcomer,"

Your grandsires toiled up Bury Hill,

    And knew the roar of " Epsom Summer : "

Their "form" was marvellous, but ne'er
    So much admired of gods and men,
As that fair form you smoothly bear
    Down Rotten Row, from eight to ten !

We jog along, a motley throng,
    Gloomy and gracious, dull and clever,
And some who find the season long,
    And some who'd make it last for ever :
One muses of a sweet shy glance,
    More eloquent than tongue or pen,
One's dreaming still of last night's dance,
    In Rotten Row, from eight to ten.

Each bears a load unguessed by each,—
    Dread of distressing Mrs. Grundy,—
Weight of an undelivered speech,—
    Doubts of the settling due on Monday.

But no ! let's ostracise Black Care,

   If ride he must, it shan't be then,

We'll leave him to a penny chair,

   In Rotten Row, from eight to ten !

ECHOES OF THE SEASON

YOUTH

" Vous en qui je salue une nouvelle aurore."

O, IT's fine to be young,
  In the warmth of the Season ;
All the Poets have sung
" O, it's fine to be young ! "
When Love's changes are rung
  Upon Folly and Reason,—
O, it's fine to be young,
  In the warmth of the Season !

IN A CORNER

" O years may come, and years may bring
  The truth that is not bliss,
But will they bring another thing
  That can compare with this?"

Ah! they sit out the dance
  In a leaf-hidden corner:
Now is Corydon's chance,—
Ah! they sit out the dance:
See her timorous glance!
  He's as pleased as Jack Horner!
Ah! they sit out the dance
  In a leaf-hidden corner!

FOLLY

"Cujus res legi non sufficit."

Not a thousand a year!
What a shock to Belgravia!

She has *married*, my dear,—

Not a thousand a year !

Did the world ever hear

    Of such selfish behaviour ?

Not a thousand a year !

What a shock to Belgravia !

DISASTER

    " Let the wilful sun
Shine westward of our window,—straight we run
A furlong's sigh as if the world were lost."

    SHE'S not asked to the Ball,

      O, Despair ! Desolation !

And it's marked "*Very* small,"

She's not asked to the Ball :

She has rushed off to call,

      But still no invitation !

She's *not* asked to the Ball,

      O, Despair ! Desolation !

"AT HOME."

" Χαῖρε, ξεῖνε · παρ' ἄμμι φιλήσεαι·

Who are those by the door?—

    Our host and our hostess?—

Never saw them before :

Who *are* those by the door?

He looks *such* an old bore,—

    She's as white as a "ghostess;"

Who are those by the door?—

    Our *host*!! and our *hostess*!!!

AT THE OPERA

" Si gaudet cantu."

There she sits in her box,—

    And is Music her passion?—

She's as cross as John Knox :

There she sits in her box.

I

" But they see one's new frocks,

And it *is* so the fashion ! "

There she sits in her box,—

And *is* Music her passion ?

ART

" Roses, you are not so fair after all ! "

HER cheek is so pink,

And it don't seem to vary :

Must we say what we think ?-

Her cheek is so pink :

From reflections we shrink,

And of comments are chary ;—

Her cheek is *so* pink,

And it *don't* seem to vary !

A QUESTION

" Methinks too little cost
  For a moment so found, so lost ! "

OUGHT the Man to be cut,
  Just as much as the Lady ?
When they've met Justice Butt,
Ought the Man to be cut ?
When they've stuck in a rut,
  Down a lane that is shady ; -
Ought the Man to be cut,
  Just as much as the Lady ?

THE END

www.ingramcontent.com/pod-product-compliance
Lightning Source LLC
Chambersburg PA
CBHW032017010726
47493CB00007B/2440